CW00420547

My Blood

A play in four acts

By A.L.L

'These people honour me with their lips, but their hearts are far from me.

They worship me in vain; their teachings are but rules taught by men.' -

Matthew 15

     "It is always with the best intentions that the worst work is done." – Oscar Wilde

 "Where we are is hell, and where hell is, there must we ever be" – Christopher Marlowe

Content Warnings: Depictions of murder, violence, bereavement; discussions of rape, human trafficking, depression, suicide, sex; religious and occult references; very strong language.

Cast List:

Adam Atreides: 55-year-old billionaire and CEO of Atreides & Co. Based on Agamemnon.

Bill Roberts: Adam's best friend, Oliver and Chloe's godfather, hedge fund advisory executive at Atreides & Co. Based on Menelaus.

Chloe Atreides (LEAD): Adam's 24-year-old daughter. Based on both Clytemnestra and Electra.

Eve Johnson (LEAD): Adam's new secretary, about 22 years old. Loosely based on the Chorus.

Jason Giordano: Chloe's 32-year-old secret boyfriend and policeman. Loosely based on Aegisthus and Medea's Jason.

Oliver Atreides (LEAD): Adam's 25-year-old son. Loosely based on Orestes.

Sandra Morgan-Leroy: Adam's 27-year-old girlfriend. Loosely based on Cassandra.

ACT I

Scene 1: Arrival

The stage is dark then a spotlight falls on the stage. Eve gets up from her seat in the audience and goes to stand in the spotlight.

Eve: There are many strange things in this world, things that go by unnoticed. Things that people would just rather not see. Ignorance is bliss, is it not?

I arrived in September 2009 to the house of Adam Atreides, a Wall Street tycoon. I had recently been selected from his apprenticeship scheme to be his new secretary. Sometimes life happens in a way where hard work really does pay off.

Lights go down. When they come back, we are in the family graveyard. Chloe stands in front of Jenny's grave, which has a white rose on top of the gravestone, facing the audience with her back to Eve. Eve approaches her.

Eve: (nervously) Excuse me.

Chloe turns around and looks at her.

Eve: My name is Eve Johnson, I'm your father's new secretary. You're his daughter, Chloe, aren't you?

Chloe: Yes.

Eve approaches and they shake hands.

Chloe: I think I've seen you somewhere before.

Eve: I moved here three weeks ago; I've been going to church in the area, you might have seen me there?

Chloe: (distractedly) Oh, yeah. That must be it.

Chloe turns back to look at her sister's grave. Eve reads the gravestone.

Eve: I'm sorry for your loss.

Chloe: (Lost in thought) Thank you. She was my little sister. She was only eleven.

Eve: I'm so sorry...I also lost my sister.

Chloe looks up at her.

It was seven years ago. She was four years older than me; we were very close too.

Chloe nods her head.

Chloe: I am sorry.

The two share a look of understanding. Pause. Chloe looks back at her sister's grave.

Eve: Can I ask, no worries if you don't want to answer, I don't want to disturb you (she looks around) but why is there a graveyard here?

Chloe: My great grandad had a taste for the extravagant, the classical. This is where all the Atreides have been buried since my ancestor arrived to America. He even dug up and flew over my ancestors' graves from Greece so we could all be here… together.

Eve: Oh nice, nice.

Beat.

Chloe: (ignoring Eve's awkwardness) You're a religious person…do you believe in Judgement Day?

Pause

Eve: W-what?

Chloe: Judgement Day. Do you believe in it?

Eve: I'm not sure. I think so? Surely everyone gets judged in the end, I guess. I don't really know.

Chloe: And what are you supposed to do when God seems to turn his eyes away?

Eve, uncomfortable, gives her a friendly but confused look.

Eve: Sorry, I don't really know what to say.

Chloe: No one ever does.

Chloe clears her throat and smiles.

Chloe: Don't mind me. We lost her around this time last year and I can't stop thinking about it… Anyway, it really is nice to meet you. Have you met Oliver yet?

Eve: No.

Chloe: Let's go introduce you, and then, I've heard, you have the pleasure of meeting everyone else at dinner tonight.

Eve chuckles politely.

Eve: Yeah. I'm looking forward to it.

Chloe: (With a friendly smile) They'll probably disappoint you, but the food won't.

Chloe kisses her fingers and tenderly touches Jenny's gravestone then beckons Eve to follow her out.

The lights fade down as they start to walk out together.

End of scene.

Scene 2: Dinner

The table is set formally but cosily with everyone close together. Sandra sits alone at the end of the table looking at her phone (Blackberry) and smoking with a bored expression on her face.

Oliver and Chloe walk in with Eve behind them.

Oliver: Sandra this is dad's new secretary – Eve Johnson.

Sandra: (Still looking at her phone) You mean new fuck.

Oliver: No need to be a bitch. Let's try and give a nice first impression, for once.

Sandra glares at Oliver. He gestures kindly to Eve to sit down; Chloe and Oliver sit next to her.

Sandra: And calling your nearly-stepmom a bitch in front of the help is a nice way to go, isn't it?

Oliver: She's not the help, she's a new friend and employee. And cut the stepmom bullshit, Sandra. (To Eve) She's only two years older than I am.

Sandra: (Piss-taking) And yet here we are. Anyway, look who's acting like a social justice warrior now. (To Eve) They're hypocrites. Campaigning to help fight drug addiction among the homeless on a Monday and snorting coke in the bathroom on a Tuesday.

Chloe: Wow. Did you just hear yourself? Is Cocaine Cassandra giving us a lecture on drugs?

Sandra: It's a metaphor, dipshit. Maybe if you'd finished college, you'd know what one is? (To Eve) They say you're their friend and they'll be nice to you now, but it won't be long before they start treating you like you're not even a person. Especially someone like you. (She shrugs her shoulders and goes back to texting on her phone) At least I'm honest.

Oliver laughs.

Oliver: You're unbelievable. You don't know the meaning of the word honesty. Don't even bother trying to act like a nice person just because Eve's here. You should just keep being yourself, an Angelina Jolie wannabe.

Sandra: Oh no, no, no, not Angelina, I'll pass on the whole adopting African kids thing, though your newly Christian sister might be into that (gestures to Chloe).

Chloe gives her a death-stare.

Sandra: I guess not.

Beat.

(To Eve, coldly) You, where are you from?

Eve: Uh, well I grew up in Detroit, I'm-

Sandra: Yeah, of course you did. I bet this place has blown your 3 dollar socks off. Bigger than your whole street put together probably?

Oliver: Enough, Cassandra. Keep your mouth shut.

Sandra: You don't talk to me like that in my own home. I will say whatever the fuck I want to, Oliver, and you will sit there and listen, or would you like your daddy to hear about this?

Chloe: I think everyone's just feeling hungry and annoyed. Let's stay calm, our starters will be here soon, and dad and Bill too probably.

Sandra: Exactly, remember whose house you're in and fucking know your place.

She smirks and takes a puff on her cigarette as two waiters come in bringing their food while Chloe sends Oliver a warning glare which means calm down and play it cool. Eve observes everything shyly and uncomfortably. They all begin eating.

Sandra: So Evie, you're from Detroit. Fuck me. I don't even want to know what it was like growing up there, though I suppose I could always watch 8 Mile if I'm bored enough. Are you a big Eminem fan? You must be.

Eve: (Politely) Well, who doesn't love Lose yourself? He's an amazing artist, and yeah, someone that comes from nothing and actually works their ass off to become super successful…they deserve the greatest respect.

Sandra: Hm, exactly. People like you and Eminem are the American Dream. Look at you now, Evie! Working for one of America's top investment banks! Even though you had to suck my boyfriend's cock to get there, I'm not judging you.

Eve and Sandra stare at each other until Adam and Bill walk in, mid-conversation, a little drunk, finding each other absolutely hilarious.

Bill: -And I told him, if you're gonna blow her off, at least make it last longer than Monaco '89.

Adam wheezes with laughter, until he catches sight of Eve and smiles at her. She smiles softly back. Sandra gazes between the two of them furiously. Oliver and Chloe don't notice this, they stare at their father, deep in thought of their own plan. Bill catches sight of the alcohol on the table and makes his way straight towards it. Adam walks to his spot at the head of the table, opposite Sandra. Eve is sitting on Adam's left, Bill on Adam's right. Chloe is sitting next to Bill and Sandra. Oliver is sitting next to Eve and Sandra.

Adam: My family. Thank you for joining me for dinner tonight. It's a special occasion. Not only are my loved ones gathered here together again, but we're here to welcome my new secretary, Eve Johnson, the first graduate of my Atreides scholarship business scheme.

While he talks, Chloe notices that Sandra is drinking water, not wine, and looks at Oliver with a discreet flash of worry. He shares her worry but sends her a look which means: Let's stay calm and continue with the plan.

Bill starts clapping after Adam stops speaking, everyone else follows. Eve bows her head shyly.

Now, it is no secret that it has been... a horrific past year for Wall Street, for the entire world, and... of course for our own family. My daughter (his voice breaks, he takes a moment to gather himself together), she is the reason that we all keep going, that we all try to live a life that would make her proud and make the world a better place. I would like to take this moment to announce the development of 15 new orphanages, kindergartens, elementary schools and college scholarships to be established in her name, in some of America's most deprived areas.

Bill starts clapping, everyone else follows, Oliver and Chloe clap very reluctantly. Adam nods and gestures for everyone to stop clapping.

Thank you. So, as I said…it's been a year from Hell. But we survived it… together, as a family. Everything I do, everything I've ever done (he quickly looks at Oliver and then looks away) has been for the family. For the Atreides. Our legacy is something greater than any of us, something that will live on far into the future. It's what makes us immortal…now, let's make a toast.

Everyone raises their glasses at Adam's request.

Adam: To the Atreides.

Everyone repeats 'the Atreides' apart from Chloe and Oliver who feel flabbergasted by their father's hypocrisy but try to play it cool. Adam quickly looks at Eve over his glass while she pretends not to see as Oliver and Chloe glance at each other subtly but conspiratorially. Sandra stares down Adam angrily and Bill just enjoys his drink. Lights fade away.

Scene 3: Dessert

When the lights come up, the family are finishing their dessert, and the atmosphere is slightly more relaxed. Bill and Adam are drinking whiskey and smoking cigars, they are more drunk, everyone else is quite sober. In the background Eve and Oliver are in the middle of having a conversation while Oliver also smokes a cigar, and Adam and Bill are having another conversation.

Sandra: I think we would've been friends if I wasn't fucking your dad. I think about this every time I'm forced to socialise with you, which, lucky for me, isn't that much anymore.

Chloe rolls her eyes and sighs.

Chloe: Why do you have to say it like that? Just say dating. I don't need the mental image in my mind.

Sandra: When's the last time you had a good fuck? Sounds like it's been ages.

Chloe: My sex life is none of your business and it's not something I want to discuss here.

Sandra: I keep forgetting that you're Christian now. Pardon me. I should say intimate relations instead, shouldn't I?

Chloe: Maybe you should stop thinking about sex full stop, for like, two seconds maybe?

Sandra: Okay Mary... but you should give me more credit. I'm not a man, I have self-control, I only think about sex when I'm in the mood for power.

Chloe: You're always in the mood for power.

Adam starts talking to Eve and Oliver, while Bill listens in.

Sandra: As are you. You think I don't notice? I see you. Your dad doesn't because he underestimates you. For a very clever man, it's quite stupid of him, but hatred is blind, isn't it? I don't underestimate you though. I know a cut-throat bitch when I see one.

Chloe stares at her with a guarded expression but then breaks it with a fake smile and takes a sip of wine. Beat. Sandra looks at her contemplatively with a small smile.

Your dad has more emotional attachment to my vagina than he's ever had to any drawing or piece of homework that you ever made for him. And my dad was the same with whoever he had his dick in at the time... It's sad, isn't it? At least you had a mom who loved you.

Chloe: I'm not interested in playing who's suffered more than who. Don't even try. Anyway, I didn't think you had any feelings. Why are you suddenly trying to be emotional with me now?

Sandra: I know, something must be wrong with me, or I must be getting old. I feel so old.

She rubs her stomach subconsciously, and stares at Adam who is talking to Eve and Oliver. She sees that Bill is sitting silently for the moment.

Switch sits with me; I want to talk to Bill.

Chloe raises her eyebrows but switches seats.

Adam: Did you know, Eve, that my son was captain of the water polo team in school and then at Yale? Our family originates from Olympia in Greece, so he really is-

Eve: A true Olympian.

Adam: Exactly! Stole the words right off my tongue. (To Bill) I told you she was smart, didn't I?

Bill breaks off talking to Sandra and shrugs. Adam and Sandra share a look.

Bill: You're never wrong, Adam. (He looks around the table) Where's the beer? I'm dying for a real drink, no more Frenchy, girly wine.

He snaps his fingers.

Where are the servants when you need em? What do you pay them thousands for? To sit in the kitchen away with the fucking fairies?

He knocks on the table and a waiter enters the room.

BEER. Now.

The waiter leaves to get him a beer.

Adam: If only your taste were more refined Bill, then I'd be able to take you to board meetings in Europe.

Bill: Don't tell me that's why you always take Mick instead. He's a clown with a dried-up pussy.

Adam: (Laughs) Language, my friend.

Bill clutches his hand to his chest.

Bill: (To Eve, in a Rah English accent) Sincerest apologies and eternal regrets, my lady.

He laughs and punches Adam playfully on the arm.

Bill: Everybody loves Adam, there's no one more charming, and no better boss in the whole U S of A. If I were to tell you all the incredible things, he's done for this country you'd be sitting here till next morning-

Oliver: Tell us.

Bill, Adam and Eve look at Oliver, he's been sitting quietly, staring into space until this moment.

Adam: What's that, champ?

Oliver looks Adam in the eye.

Oliver: I think Eve would want to hear about all the incredible things you've done for this country. So Bill should tell us.

Adam smiles.

Adam: Ollie's always been my biggest fan. I remember when he was a baby and would follow me around, copying my walk, holding a tootsie roll like a cigar. He's my pride, my heir. Don't give me all the credit son, you've been working for me for four years now. Why don't you tell Eve about some of our philanthropic work?

Oliver takes a sip of wine and smirks bitterly.

Oliver: Well there's just been so much, especially in the past couple years, I wouldn't know where to begin. You'd think with the Crash we'd have cut down but oh no, nothing could ever stop Atreides and Co., not even death itself.

Bill laughs to diffuse the tension.

Bill: I think he means that we're lucky, Eve. Really fucking lucky. Colleagues and friends lost everything, even took their own lives, but we managed to stay afloat, ride out the tide, even emerge more successful –

Chloe: (Cutting in from across the table) It wasn't luck. Don't be so humble, Bill. The only reason we're still sitting here today, enjoying this fine Chateau Cheval Blanc is because of you, and of course, my brilliant dad.

Chloe raises her glass to him.

Adam: You shouldn't be raising your glass to me. You should be raising it to your husband. He's the only reason you are still sitting at my table. When's the last time you even cared to see him?

Chloe scowls.

Chloe: We're still separated dad; nothing's changed since the last time you asked.

Adam rolls his eyes.

Adam: I don't think you should bother showing up here next time without him.

Chloe: He's a fucking redneck.

Adam bangs his hand on the table. Everyone goes still.

Adam: He's what you deserve, you fucking brat. Do you think you could ever have worked at America's top investment bank, being the college-fucking-dropout that you are, if you weren't the daughter of the man who runs it? Go get a degree, get your own job, live off your own money, not mine, not your husband's, who I found for you might I add, and then sit there and complain about your life.

Chloe: Yes, you did find me my husband. My lovely brothel and child-porn addicted husband. (To Eve) So he's a top guy in Hollywood, of course. (To Adam) But I'm not quite sure 'find' is the right word. Forced me to marry him as a plan b to financially secure our bank would be more accurate. I was happy to give you and Bill all the credit, but if you want to bring up everything that was sacrificed for Atreides and Co to still exist, fine, let's do that.

Adam: (Calmly) Get out.

Everyone is silent. Chloe doesn't move. Bill laughs to diffuse the tension.

Bill: I'm sure she's just kidding, Adam, we're all just hammered and kidding around, aren't we? I can't be the only one –

Adam: (Ignoring Bill and continuing) Your face makes me sick. Get out. I will never invite you into my home again.

Oliver: What about me?

Adam: Shut up. This doesn't concern you.

Oliver: If she leaves, I leave.

Adam sighs in frustration.

Adam: Why am I cursed with such fucking annoying children?

He takes a swig of wine and then rubs his temples, starting to look more tired. Bill yawns. Oliver leans across the table and touches his father's wrist.

Oliver: I'm sorry dad. Bill's right. We're just kidding. Next family dinner Chloe will bring Randy and I'll finally get a girlfriend, like you wanted, and bring her along too.

Adam: (Yawning) Good. It's good that you've come to your senses, Oliver. I forgive you, because I am grace itself, and because you, son, are the apple of my fucking eye.

Oliver smiles bitterly to himself.

Oliver: I thought that was Jenny.

Adam glares at him, caught off guard. Oliver stands up, says goodnight to Eve and walks out.

Bill yawns loudly.

Bill: You know what Adam; I'm starting to feel really fucking run down. I might crash too.

Adam: You can fuck off then. I'll catch you in the morning.

Bill: You better, you owe me a round of golf remember?

Adam: Yes, yes (Adam waves him away with his hand, Bill leaves the room)

Adam: (To Chloe) Am I in Hell? Why the fuck are you still sitting here?

Chloe gets up, Eve also tries to get up and leave but Adam tells her to stay. Chloe whispers something in her ear then leaves.

Sandra keeps sitting, staring at her nails. Eve looks down at her empty plate awkwardly.

Adam: (To Sandra) Baby, what were you talking about to Bill? You know I don't like it when you talk to him.

Sandra sighs.

Sandra: Nothing important. What were you talking about to your little parasite? (She nods at Eve when she says the word parasite).

Adam chuckles.

Adam: I'll see you later, sweetie. Eve and I need to do some admin work before the Paris call tomorrow. It won't be long, I promise, but don't disturb me, you know I hate being disturbed when I'm working.

Beat.

Sandra: Well, you better be working very hard then.

Sandra gets up, kisses Adam on the way out and leaves.

Adam stares at Eve. She slowly raises her eyes to meet his eyes and smiles while the lights fade away.

Act II

Scene 1: Retribution

This scene takes place in Adam's office. When the lights come up, we see Adam Atreides tied to his chair. He is drugged & fast asleep at his desk with his head on the table. Oliver and Chloe watch him.

Oliver: I can't believe we're really doing this.

Chloe says nothing, she walks up behind Adam and checks if he's still breathing, then prods and shakes him to check how awake he is.

Chloe: Wow. He's completely knocked out…why does he have to look so innocent when he's asleep?

Oliver shifts uncomfortably and then starts pacing, visibly distressed. Chloe watches him, looking like she's holding back tears.

Oliver stops abruptly.

Oliver: Maybe this is a bad idea. I don't know if I can do this.

Chloe: Me too.

She looks at Adam.

Chloe: We've been planning it for ages, but now that we're actually here…it's weird, but I kind of forgot he was a living, breathing human…rather than something untouchable. D'you know what I mean?

Chloe walks over to the hunting knives displayed on the bookshelf. There are two. She takes them both and holds one in each hand, staring at them.

Chloe: Grandad's Cretan knives.

She turns around to look at Oliver.

Chloe: I don't know what's right or wrong anymore. All I know is that our sister died scared and suffering because of the person meant to always protect her.

She puts the knives down on the desk in front of their father.

Chloe: Ollie, I don't know what to do.

There's a soft knock on the door.

Chloe and Oliver look at each other worried.

Oliver: Who is it?

Eve: Eve.

Oliver walks over to the door, composes himself then unlocks it, but when he opens the door, he stands in the doorway in such a way that Eve's view into the room is blocked.

Oliver: Hello Eve, what are you doing here?

Eve: Oliver, I'm sorry to disturb, but I need to talk to you. It's urgent.

Oliver: Now's not the best time Eve, dad's drunk and I'm looking after him. Maybe tomorrow morning? Sorry.

He starts to close the door, but Eve stops him.

Eve: Oliver, I know.

Oliver: Know what?

Eve: About what really happened to Jenny.

Chloe comes to door.

Chloe: What do you mean?

Eve: We should talk inside, so that no one overhears.

Chloe: Tell us a bit of what you know first.

Eve: Her death wasn't a random case of kidnapping. Your father was involved. And your godfather, Bill Roberts.

Oliver tenses. He pulls Eve inside and quickly closes the door. Eve sees Adam asleep at his desk and notices the knives.

Oliver: What do you want?

Eve composes herself.

Eve: It's me. I'm the one that sent you the anonymous emails, Chloe, with pictures of the cult, from the night of Jenny's murder.

Beat.

Chloe: How is that possible?

Eve: I've been investigating them for years since my sister was killed in the exact same circumstances as your sister Jenny. It was also written off by the police as a freak attack.

Eve moves to sit in the armchair next to Adam's desk and stares at him and the knives as she does so.

We were really poor, and she got involved with the wrong people. They trafficked her. I found a connection between your family name and the sex ring she ended up in.

I knew it was destiny when Adam opened up his programme and I saw a way to get directly into your family...and take my revenge.

Chloe: But why did you send me the photos of that night, if you were planning to take your own revenge?

Eve: I didn't just move here three weeks ago, I've been watching all of you for months. I knew you were grieving your sister and thought you should know the truth.

Oliver: You were stalking us, you mean?

Eve: Yes. But wouldn't you if you were trying to take revenge on your sister's killers?

Chloe: We didn't kill your sister.

Eve: No. But your father did. And Bill. And their cult...do you know why?

Oliver: Because they're sick bastards and... satanists.

Chloe holds her cross.

Eve: If you'd have told me three years ago that an elite group of satanists existed and that they killed people in ritual sacrifices for money and power I'd have thought you were a crazy conspiracy theorist...but here we all are, suffering because of those people in the shadows.

Chloe: I still don't know if I exactly believe in the whole black magic part. But the photos were fucking creepy. It was like... the KKK meets one of those supernatural horror movies -

Eve: Unfortunately, it's very real.

Chloe: I believe that the cult exists, our father was involved in many dodgy illegal activities, I guess satanism is hardly a stone's throw away when you've already sold your soul for cash. And we saw his face and Bill's in the photos, and the way it was all covered up...we believe you, Eve.

Oliver: In the photos, all the other members were disguised in masks and cloaks though. But we can assume that at least some of them also ran in our father's circles.

Chloe: After we take care of our father, we'll hunt them down and expose them too.

Eve nods, in thought.

Eve: So what are you planning to do with Adam then?

They all look at Adam.

Oliver: Chloe thought we should stab him. So that he could suffer like Jenny did.

Chloe: Why are you singling me out? I thought you agreed.

Oliver: I thought I did. But it's so violent, Chloe. Are you really prepared to stick a knife in your own dad? Wishing someone dead and actually doing it, are two different things.

Chloe is silent.

Eve: I'd be hesitant too. But then I remember the rape bruises that were found on my sister-

Oliver: Our sister wasn't raped.

Eve: Can you be sure? Didn't the police report say that she was so cut up, she was only identified by the bracelet they found near her body?

Oliver and Chloe grimace. Chloe starts crying.

Oliver: Our dad was a monster, but even he wouldn't have gone that far.

He goes silent. Eve watches him.

Eve: Forgive me, I'm speaking what I know happened to my sister and other previous victims of the cult. I'm still haunted by the images on her police file. The sixty-six stab marks. The dismembered limbs. And then, I remember all the innocent people that died scared and tortured. There's no real justice in the world, and there never was. People like your father will never stop because this world is built for them. Not for the normal people who stand in their way. How many more young women and men, children, will have their lives ruined? Who's going to step up and do something about it? Sometimes you have to do one bad thing so that a lot of good can follow.

Oliver looks at Eve in surprise because Adam used to say the same thing.

Especially when the law, meant to protect you, meant to protect your children, fails you. This isn't murder. It's retribution. It's doing what the legal system should be doing if it was there to actually protect its citizens. Are you going to look the other way? Or are you going to do something selfless, for once in your life? Because if you don't stop your father, no one else will.

Eve pauses and takes out a small clear vial from her pocket. She puts it in Chloe's hand.

Eve: This is how I was planning to kill him. It's painless and untraceable. Do what you think is right… he may be your father but people like him don't deserve to exist. You'll be doing the world a favour - he's too dangerous.

Chloe stares at the bottle with tears in her eyes.

Chloe: (Crying) You're right… (under her breath) my baby sister.

She bursts into tears. Oliver hugs her. They hold each other and sob.

Chloe: (Still hugging Oliver) They made her suffer so much. I can't even think about it.

Oliver: (Crying) And dad did it to his own daughter.

Chloe pushes out of the hug, she puts the vial in her pocket, walks over to the knives and takes them.

Chloe: It's not fair that he'd die so easily when Jenny died in such agony. He has to suffer too. It won't even be half of what she went through.

Chloe hands Oliver a knife. He takes it.

Oliver: Let me do it. Alone. I don't want you to have the blood on your hands, Chlo.

Chloe: No. If we're doing this. We're doing it together.

Oliver: Chloe –

Chloe: We don't have all night. We've already been talking for too long-

Oliver: You stab once, and I'll do the rest. You're doing no more than that.

She walks over to her father. Oliver follows her. The lights dim and change to red. They quickly put on chemical gloves. Chloe and Oliver look at each other and, with the hand that is empty, hold hands briefly over their father's sleeping body. Then Oliver raises his knife and stabs Adam in the back. Adam starts twitching. Oliver holds him down and stabs him more while Chloe looks on, frozen. Eve watches from the side. The lights fade out as he stabs Adam.

Scene 2: Disaster

When the lights come up Chloe is helping Oliver clean himself up because he's covered in blood. Eve stands outside the door on guard duty, she paces about in agitation. Suddenly we hear 'It's Britney Bitch' as Gimme More plays in the distance from Sandra's iPod. It catches Eve off guard, and she accidentally knocks over a vase on display next to her. Sandra hears the noise and comes storming down the corridor.

Sandra: (Seeing Eve, absolutely furious) What the fuck, what the fuck are you doing here at 3am, you fucking whore!

Eve: No, no, no, Sandra, please, I can explain. Adam asked me to wait out here, he's working on notes for the next –

Sandra: You couldn't even wait one night. One fucking night before you started fucking him. Let me through –

Eve blocks Sandra from entering.

Eve: It's not like that, I swear. You can't go in there, Adam strictly said he wasn't to be disturbed, even by you –

Sandra: (exploding) Fuck off!

She slaps Eve and shoves her to the floor. She takes out a key from her dressing gown pocket and unlocks the door to the office while shouting at Adam. Meanwhile, Chloe and Oliver have been hearing the commotion and panicking. They try to untie Adam from the chair and place him on the floor behind the desk but can't undo the knots on the rope. They then lie him down carefully with the chair behind the desk and run forward to sit in front of it.

Sandra walks in. Meanwhile:

Sandra: - and I will not be fucking disrespected like this, oh! (She sees Chloe and Oliver)

What are you two doing here? Where's Adam?

Oliver: He went out.

Sandra: Where?

Eve comes into the room rubbing her face. She shoots Oliver and Chloe an apologetic look. Sandra doesn't turn round.

Chloe: How are we supposed to know? He never talks business with us anymore.

Sandra: (Seeing a bit of blood on Oliver) Why do you – (she notices that there's blood dripping under the table) What the –

She storms round the table as Chloe and Oliver leap up to stop her. She sees Adam and screams. She tries to run for her life, hysterical, but Chloe and Oliver stop her and wrestle her into the armchair next to the desk. Eve leaves the room to look around for something they can use as a rope. Oliver punches Sandra in the face and knocks her out. Lights fade away.

Scene 3: Catch-22

When the lights come up Sandra sits tied up and gagged. Chloe and Oliver stand in front of her, and Eve stands off to the side.

Oliver: Thank you for finding the rope, Eve, please could you leave us and go and check that Bill is actually asleep? He's been drugged too, so he should be. Don't wake him up.

Eve: Yeah, I'm so sorry guys (she gestures to Sandra)

Chloe: Don't worry. We all just need to stay calm now.

Eve nods and leaves the room.

Oliver: (To Sandra) You need to let us explain. We had to tie you up and shut you up so you could hear us out for a moment. I'm sorry I punched you in the face.

Sandra, even though she's terrified, still glares at him.

Chloe: We aren't sadists. We killed dad because he and Bill killed Jenny, with their satanic cult, in exchange for stopping our bank from going Lehman Brothers.

Sandra raises her eyebrows.

Chloe: You don't have to believe us. But it's the truth. We had to do this, because no one else was going to stop him, and he was too dangerous to be kept alive. You don't know how many bad things he's done.

Oliver and Chloe glance at each other.

Oliver: We're going to remove your gag now. So that we can talk, calmly, as adults. Don't make us regret it.

Oliver removes the gag.

Sandra: (Crying) You fucking animals. You killed your own dad, you killed my Adam. What the fuck is wrong with you?

She sobs.

Chloe: Did you hear none of what we just said? He killed Jenny.

Sandra: I don't give a fuck about your sister. You two are monsters. Fucking monsters.

Oliver: (Calmly) Enough. We can go round in circles complaining about who's worse than who. It doesn't matter. Sandra let's discuss your silence, and how you're going to pretend you've seen and know nothing, for the rest of your life.

Sandra: You mean… you're not going to kill me too?

Oliver: Of course not. Because we're not monsters.

Sandra relaxes an inch.

Sandra: Okay. Let's say I believe you…anyway, you couldn't kill me even if you wanted to, after what I'm about to tell you.

Chloe: And what's that?

Sandra: I'm pregnant… and you wouldn't kill your future sibling, right? Because you're not monsters.

Chloe: You're lying.

Sandra: Why do you think I haven't been drinking recently? Well I guess neither of you come over enough to notice, but I didn't drink at dinner, did I?

Oliver: Yeah, but you smoked.

Sandra: Well you can't expect me to give up both drinking and smoking. I'm not Mother Teresa.

Oliver puts his head in hands. Chloe sits on the edge of the desk in a bit of shock. Sandra smirks.

Sandra: Ha. You know I'm telling the truth now, motherfuckers… I'll be silent. But I want money and child support.

Chloe guides Oliver to the corner of the room so that they can talk more privately.

Chloe: What do we do?

Oliver: We'll have to pay her off like she wants.

Chloe: But what if we write her a check and she keeps it and then still goes to the police?

Oliver: I don't think so. Cos if she does that, she's not getting any more money from us in the future.

Chloe: Okay… what if we give her, like, 300 million now, with the condition that she never contacts us again.

Oliver: 300 million?! Jesus Christ, Chloe. No, she'll just take all that money and a few years later contact us with some excuse about why she needs more. And we'll have to say yes because we aren't in a position to be making conditions.

Chloe: So, what do we do? Just let her blackmail us for the rest of our lives? Be at her fucking mercy? No. She'll make our lives hell.

Oliver: What choice do we have Chloe? We'll have to keep paying her. Even if we run dry. Because I don't want no more blood on our hands. No more killing. Our money's cursed anyway. It's what Jenny paid her life with.

Chloe: She hates us. She'll make us into her own personal puppets because she's a fucking, sadistic bitch. The money is going to become our curse if we let her have so much control over our lives.

Oliver: Then what are you suggesting?

Chloe: I… I don't know.

Pause. Chloe turns around and walks over to Adam's desk. She gets out his check book and pen and walks over to Sandra.

Chloe: 10 million.

Sandra laughs in her face.

Sandra: That's nothing to you. And nothing near how much this palace of a house costs. 100 million.

Chloe: Why do you even need that much? You're a Morgan-Leroy. You're not lacking on money.

Sandra: But I am, Chloe. (She sighs.) My father was in severe gambling debt. He left the little he had to his Brazilian bikini model whores, my bitch mother and aunt disowned me long ago and my sisters won't help me, not after I fucked both of their husbands...but how is it my fault they decided to pick up my leftovers? Anyway, long story short, I've got no inheritance and no family.

Beat.

Oliver: You kept that quiet.

Sandra: Your father knew. No one else needed to...I cannot be poor. It's not who I am. It's not who I'm meant to be. I'd rather kill myself.

Oliver: Well, you'd be doing us a favour.

Chloe: You're getting confident that we won't kill you. We could... fucking - take you out, put you somewhere no one's gonna find you. After all, you've got no one who cares about you. No one would know.

Sandra rolls her eyes.

Sandra: Please stop trying to act gangster Chloe, you're too cringe, and I know that you won't kill me because for how much you go on and on and on about how much you loved your Jenny, you'd be a hypocrite and evil to kill your new baby sibling, wouldn't you? 85 million.

Chloe: 60

Sandra: 80

Chloe: 65

Sandra: 70

Chloe: Done.

Chloe scribbles a check and then tosses it in Sandra's lap.
Sandra smiles.

Sandra: Well, my dear kids. I think you should untie me now,
don't you? Hurry the fuck up.

Chloe and Oliver pause, fury on their faces, but they go untie
her. They say the following lines while they untie her. Sandra
caresses her wrists and then strokes her belly.

Oliver: Did dad know you were pregnant?

Sandra: Not yet.

Chloe snorts.

Chloe: When exactly were you planning to tell him?

Sandra: What does it matter now? He's gone. Ow!

Sandra kicks Oliver.

Watch it! I have delicate ankles, and my feet are sore all the time now I'm pregnant, massage my toes.

Oliver stares at her.

Do it, bitch.

Oliver sighs and starts rubbing her feet.

(To Chloe) You, go get me some water. I could drink a fucking river.

Chloe goes over to pour some water from the jug into a cup. She does this as slowly as she can.

Oliver: We're blaming the murder on Bill. They had an argument, which developed since dinner and the jealousy he'd been harbouring for years over Adam stealing you from him made him explode, he stabbed him in a fit of rage…Go up to your room and sleep. Make sure you have your best acting skills on tomorrow when the housekeeper comes in and discovers his body and then when we call the police and deal with the murder investigation and trial. You can fuck off once it's all over.

Sandra: Don't worry, I'm not stupid. You can trust me to do my part. Of course I might need some incentives to keep me going. The Oscar-worthy acting you're asking of me would be enough to exhaust di Caprio, let alone a pregnant woman.

After she says 'oscar- worthy acting', Chloe hands the water to Oliver.

Sandra: You two really tried so hard to plan this all out, didn't you? Till I came and fucked it up. (Shrugs) That's life though.

She snaps her fingers at Oliver, and he passes her the water. She gulps it down.

You lose some… (She picks up her check and smirks as she looks at it) You win some. (She winks) Pleasure doing business with you bitches, I'll see you tomorrow morning.

She blows a kiss to Oliver and Chloe and then starts to walk out, but she very suddenly starts to feel unwell while she nears the door. She collapses in the doorway. Oliver and Chloe turn around when they hear her fall.

Oliver: What the fuck?

Oliver rushes over and bends down to check on her. The lights fade out to black as he does this.

ACT III

Scene 1: Downfall

The stage is dark apart from a spotlight on Eve like in the very first scene of the play.

Eve: When the housekeeper arrived the next morning, she was given a horrible shock to find not one, but two dead bodies. The first, her mistress, Miss Cassandra Morgan-Leroy, dead in the doorway of Adam's study. The coroner could find no traces of foul play, her heart had simply seemed to stop beating. It was ruled to be a heart attack from the shock of seeing her boyfriend stabbed to death, and no further investigation was taken by the police.

The second body the housekeeper came across was her employer's - Adam Atreides. Stabbed seven times in his back, (Eve laughs bitterly) …. Chloe, Oliver, Bill and I were all immediately taken in for police questioning on suspicion of murder.

Eve leaves the stage. Spotlight on a metal table and two chairs. We are at the police station. Bill and Jason enter the room. Bill looks bored, Jason gestures for him to sit down and then sits opposite him. Bill sits and starts tapping his foot impatiently. Jason switches on a recorder.

Jason: Questioning of Bill Andrew Chad Roberts III. Suspect of the homicide of Adam Atreides…Mr Roberts, may I call you Bill?

Bill: No.

Jason: Mr Roberts, where were you at 3am on Tuesday the 21st of September, the estimated time of the attack?

Bill: I was fucking asleep.

Jason: In Adam Atreides' house, correct?

Bill sighs impatiently.

Bill: (patronisingly) Yes.

Jason: Why were you at Mr Atreides' house?

Bill: Because I was staying over, Adam invited me to come the day before he died. We had a family dinner party on the 20th and then I went to bed, fucked out of my mind drunk.

Jason: Can you recall the conversations that took place at dinner on the 20th?

Bill: Yeah, I guess.

Jason: What did you talk about?

Bill: Golf, college days…. How is this relevant?

Jason: You are under legal obligation to comply with police questioning, Mr Roberts. Can you remember what else was spoken of between you and Adam Atreides at dinner?

Bill: Look, boy, someone (waggles his finger in Jason's face) clearly didn't read my file properly, you know, I went to Yale.

Jason: Congratulations. Now, can you explain why-

Bill: No, no, no. I don't think you understand. I wasn't just one of those average Bradleys that go to Yale. I went to Yale in an exclusive way.

Jason: I don't follow.

Bill: Well of course you don't, it's beyond someone like you. But if you go and tell my name to your superiors, they'll get the right idea, and you'll be saving everyone a lot of time.

Bill leans back in his chair.

Off you go, Kiddo.

Jason: Mr Roberts, what you are implying is entirely inappropriate. If you refuse to comply with police enquiry you will be considered as withholding information, which is a criminal offence.

Bill: Don't try and fool me. I know my rights; I have the right to remain silent. I refuse to talk without my lawyer present.

Jason: Actually, your lawyer was contacted but he decided to terminate representing you.

Jason shows him a sheet of paper with proof of contract resignation. Bill starts to feel a little more on edge but hides it.

Bill: Well, you'll have to wait until I get a new one then. I am a citizen of this country; born and raised. I have the right to a lawyer. I refuse to speak without one.

Jason: That is fine, but my only concern is that there may be no lawyer left in the US willing to represent you. Your previous lawyer cited intimidation and abuse as reasons for his resignation.

Bill laughs.

Bill: Bullshit. Complete bullshit. I have an excellent relationship with my lawyer. Someone must have paid that back-stabbing, slimy bastard off. (patronisingly) Have you thought about how it might be the same person who's trying to frame me for killing my best friend? Adam was…a brother to me, why would I…look at you trying to trick me into talking! You think you can one-up me, boy? Who the fuck are you? Some foetus that just crawled out the crib trying to be… Hercule fucking Poirot?

Jason: You used to be in a relationship with Miss Cassandra Morgan-Leroy, before she started dating your former boss, Adam Atreides, five years ago. How long were you two together for?

Bill is silent. He gives Jason the finger and death- stares him.

Jason: Because Mrs Chloe Atreides told us in police questioning that you and Cassandra had an on and off sexual relationship which spanned several years, since you took her virginity when she was sixteen.

Bill looks at him, flabbergasted.

Bill: That is none of your business and completely irrelevant. And an entirely inappropriate way to talk about a woman, a recently deceased woman as well.

Jason: You would have been forty-four at the time you first had intercourse with her, when she was still a minor, is that correct?

Pause.

Bill: Chloe's lying - she's a bitch. I never touched Sandy; I mean Sandra.

Jason: I have pictures of you and Sandra together embracing. Several people in your circle and many acquaintances have all confirmed that you used to date. It's common knowledge, Bill. There's no point trying to deny it. You started engaging in sexual relations with her when she was still a minor, is that correct?

Bill: Absolutely not. (He sighs in frustration) Listen boy, okay, yes, we used to date. But Sandra, was not a virgin when we first slept together, believe me. We first slept together when she was legal, she was nineteen, and very, very experienced.

Jason: How long did your relationship last?

Silence.

Jason: Chloe Atreides told me that it lasted three years, until Cassandra met Adam at his 50th birthday party and then left you immediately for him instead. Apparently, you walked in on them having intercourse in his study. That must have been very shocking and hurtful for you, Bill, to see your girlfriend and your best friend betraying you like that.

Silence.

Jason: Do you agree with Chloe's version of events? You were in a relationship with Sandra until she left you the day of Adam's 50th birthday party?

Bill: (Impulsively) No. No I don't agree. Because Sandy – Sandra, and I, what we had was hardly a relationship. She had a bit of a reputation you see - everyone had a ride. It was a purely sexual, very, very casual fling. That was it. So no, it didn't hurt me when she switched to Adam. I had no hard feelings for either of them.

Jason: Do you write love letters to all your casual flings then, Bill?

Bill: (incredulously) What?

Jason takes a piece of paper and reads (he cringes at the particularly cringey parts while he reads it). Bill's eyes grow wider and wider in utter shock as he realises that Jason is reading out a private diary entry he made five years ago.

Jason: (reading) 'My dearest Sandy, I ache for your lips and your pussy. Every time I see you, I want to make you wetter than Niagara Falls. You belong to me. To me. I've never been stabbed so deeply in the back before. You, my love, with my best friend. He's always had a selfish side, but I never thought he would do this to me. We always had each other's backs! Us against the world! But I guess not. He thinks he can do whatever he likes. Well one day, one day he'll regret fucking me over like this…'

Jason clears his throat and puts down the letter on the table. Bill grabs it and analyses it, trying to work out in his mind how Jason could have possibly gotten his diary entry. Meanwhile Jason talks…

Jason: That's quite the letter there, Bill… 'I've never been stabbed so deeply in the back before'. 'One day, he'll regret fucking me over like this'. Is that why you waited so long to take your revenge? You waited for the perfect moment, and then you stabbed Adam Atreides seven times in his back?

Bill: (furiously) I never fucking wrote this! (He waves the sheet of paper) Lies! Fucking lies!

He throws Jason's folder on the floor. Jason sighs calmly.

Jason: Please refrain from trying to implement intimidating and abusive behaviour, Mr Roberts. It seems your lawyer must have been correct.

Bill: (Trying to contain his explosive anger) Oh you are going to fucking regret talking to me like this, boy. Mark my words… (gesturing to the letter) it's a forgery. I never sent Sandra any letters.

Beat.

Have you been in my house? Have you looked through all my things?

Jason: Now what would give you that impression?

Jason smiles.

Jason: But I don't think your attack on Mr Atreides was planned out. It was frantic, emotional. Done impulsively. It was to do with the Paris deal, wasn't it? The Paris deal you disagreed with and told him not to sign. That's what drove you off the edge, the fact that Adam was going to let you down, again.

Bill shakes his head.

Bill: Lies. (He laughs incredulously) Lies. (Beat.) Don't worry, I don't expect someone like you to understand the truth. I don't know who the fuck you think you are, but you clearly don't know who you're dealing with. (Patronisingly) You are going to regret this.

Jason: You thought the Paris deal was foolish and risky, didn't you? It was going to put your personal finances in danger again. And after the Crash, you didn't think it was the time to be taking any more risks.

Bill: Adam is - was, a brother to me, we knew each other for a bit more than forty years now. We went to school together, then college, I am his children's godfather, I watched them grow up. We're family. Yeah, we had our petty disagreements, and he did things which made me pissed, but that's what family does. No girl, no business deal could ever make me want to kill him.

Jason nods and switches off the recording.

Jason: Thank you for your compliance in today's questioning. I will do my best to find a lawyer willing to represent you.

Lights fade away.

Scene 2: The Lovers

When the lights come up Jason and Chloe are holding each other. Chloe's eyes are closed as she hugs Jason. She feels, briefly, at peace. Jason rubs her back gently.

Jason: He's such an ass. I can't wait to see him sentenced. You should've heard the way he kept shoving Yale down my throat like it was the answer to everything. These people really think the whole world belongs to them, don't they?

Chloe: (She sighs) Yeah.

She gazes up at him.

Chloe: You think he will get sentenced then?

Jason: I'm afraid I'm not at liberty to discuss the private details of a case with anyone. No matter how beautiful they are.

He holds her face and kisses her cheek.

How devious.

Chloe raises her eyebrows. He kisses her other cheek.

How sexy.

He reaches down to kiss her lips. Chloe lightly grazes his lips with hers then turns her head away just as he's about to kiss her. She laughs.

Chloe: Neither are you at liberty to sleep with one of your suspects, but that didn't stop you.

He kisses her hair playfully.

You're so corny. What will I do with you?

Jason: You mean to say what would you do without me?

Chloe: I'd be lost! And you'd be left without anyone to torture you -

Jason: Oh I'd die of boredom then, but having to hear Bill speak again might just torture me to death first, (he smirks) in a different way -

Chloe winces.

Chloe: Let's stop talking about death. I can't bear it.

Jason: I'm sorry babe. I thought we were just kidding around.

Chloe: No, no, it's fine. It's just all been a lot.

Jason: I understand. (He interlaces his fingers with hers and says softly) How are you feeling?

Chloe: I wish people would stop asking me that. I don't want to think about how I feel. I want to forget everything… I wish we could just get on a plane to Rome. Promise me you'll take me there after this is all over?

Jason: Will we still be together when this is all over?

Chloe: What do you mean?

Jason: I'm not an idiot, Chlo, but I'm scared of letting you make me into one. Your family always uses people and then tosses them to the curb when they're done with them. How do I know you won't do the same to me?

Chloe cups his face in her hands and brings him close. She runs her thumb gently over his bottom lip and then talks.

Chloe: Since I lost Jenny, you and Ollie have been all I have. I don't think there are many good people in this world. But then I remember the two of you, and it makes the sky a bit less grey.

Jason smiles.

Jason: Who's the corny one now?

Chloe playfully punches him in the chest.

Chloe: (Laughing) I was trying to say something meaningful, Jason!

Jason: (Laughing) I'm sorry. Just trying to make you laugh. It's good to see that again.

Chloe smiles then suddenly gets serious as she remembers something.

Chloe: One thing J, you know Eve? She's the one that sent me the photos of the cult from that night. But what I'm wondering is, how did she get them? She says she's been investigating them for years, but still.

Jason: Have you asked her?

Chloe: Haven't had the chance to ask her in private.

Jason: Well you have had a crazy few days… I'll look into it. Don't worry. I'm also on my way to discovering who else was there that night. But I gotta be honest with you, Chloe. I think we're getting into dangerous territory here. Whoever these people are, they're powerful. Very, very powerful…I don't want to end up dead because I asked too many questions.

Chloe: Jason don't be silly.

Jason: No, Chloe. Don't try and bullshit me. You need to take these people seriously.

Chloe: Well it's hard to completely do that when, right now, they're just a shadow, which is why you need to keep going. So that we know who we're dealing with.

She tugs him towards her.

Chloe: (Cheekily) You're my hero.

Jason: Fuck off.

He kisses her. Lights fade out.

INTERVAL.

ACT IV

Scene 1: Climax

Stage goes dark. Spotlight on Eve.

Eve: The trial went surprisingly smoothly. Bill was found guilty and sentenced to a lifetime in prison. He's still sitting there now, believing that the cult will come and save him... We couldn't believe how easy it had all been. It didn't feel right. It felt almost as if, well, as if we were being allowed to get away with it...

Eve takes out a letter from her coat and holds it up to the audience.

We all received one of these the next morning, which confirmed our fears.

She reads out the letter.

'To Eve Johnson, daughter of Sarah Johnson of Apartment 3B, North Street, Belmont, Detroit.

We would like to offer our condolences over the tragic homicide of your former employer Mr Adam Atreides. Please be aware that the case has been closed and any further investigation into the activities of Mr Atreides or Mr Roberts past will not be tolerated. Your mother likes to go to Frankie's every Tuesday night, if you want her to continue to do so, and yourself remain free instead of a convicted accessory to murder, cease your searching now.'

It was unsigned but it came with the same symbol that was on Adam's ring. The three of us agreed to meet the next morning to discuss what to do.

Stage goes dark.

When the lights come up, we are in a lounge room in Adam's house with a couch, coffee table and armchair. There is a bowl of red apples on the coffee table. Oliver sits on the couch and Chloe in the armchair next to the door, they sit silently, deep in thought.

Chloe: So we aren't going read each other's letters then?

Oliver: I'm not showing you mine.

Chloe: Why not?

Oliver: (agitated) Because I can't. Why don't you show me yours?

Chloe: (annoyed) Because I can't.

Oliver shrugs his shoulders and looks away. He fidgets uncomfortably.

Oliver: What are you going to do about the cult?

Chloe: Why do I have to do anything?

Oliver: I mean…I thought you wanted to expose them.

Chloe: I thought that's what you wanted too, Oliver, why are you making me the one in charge?

She gets up and paces around.

Oliver: Did they threaten you?

She pauses and looks at him.

Chloe: Yes.

Oliver: Do you believe them? That they'll do it.

Chloe: They knew things I don't understand how they could have known (she looks around the room afraid) do you think there are cameras? Do you think they put cameras in our house?

Oliver looks around him, also afraid. There's a knock at the door and they both jump, scared. They don't say anything and look at the door in fear.

Eve: Hello? It's me.

They both breathe a sigh of relief.

Chloe: Eve, come in.

Eve opens the door and walks in; she notices that they look on edge.

Eve: Are you guys alright?

Chloe: Yeah. We're good…do you have your letter?

Eve nods, takes it out from her coat and chucks it on the coffee table.

Eve: They know where my mom lives, even her routine.

Chloe and Oliver read the letter. Eve notices the apples on the table and chuckles to herself, she takes an apple, bites into it and plonks herself down in the armchair. She sits there, relaxed, like she owns the room.

Oliver stops reading the letter first and looks at Eve, he thinks she seems different but can't work out why. When she meets his eye, he looks away. Then she looks at Chloe.

Eve: By the way Chloe, Jason's outside, he says that he has to speak to you, and it's urgent.

Chloe: (To Oliver) It must be about the letters, he hasn't been picking up my calls - he better explain why. I'll be back.

She leaves the room. Eve watches her go and then smiles at Oliver.

Eve: Apple?

Oliver shakes his head.

Oliver: No thanks.

Oliver and Eve freeze as the part of the stage that they are on goes dark. We see Chloe and Jason walking up to Jenny's grave where they stop to talk.

Chloe: Here we are, somewhere where we won't be overheard. Now talk - why are you being so mysterious?

Jason glances over his shoulder then turns back to Chloe.

Jason: We need to talk about two things…firstly, I've decided to break up with you.

Chloe stares at him with an expression that gives: 'bitch, what?'

Jason: (Ignoring her expression and continuing) Second, as a token of good will, I'm leaving you with a gift, a list of everyone that was there the night Jenny… (he trails off awkwardly as he looks at her grave) but I warn you, you mi-

Chloe: What the actual fuck? Are you seriously breaking up with me? And are you seriously doing it by my dead sister's grave too? What the fuck is wrong with you?

Jason: What, did you expect the waterworks? Sorry your majesty, but I'm not as dumb as you think I am. You're the daughter of a billionare. I'm the son of truck driver from the Bronx. The relationship was only ever gonna last as long as you had use for me. And if not me,

you'd have slept with any policeman you thought you could manipulate. You don't have the right to act upset with me, cos you never even loved me. I only went along with it because I had my own reasons.

Chloe: And what reasons were they?

Jason smiles.

Jason: I am the one who sent the photos of your father and Bill from that night to Eve. In fact, I'm the one who took them.

Chloe and Jason freeze as their part of the stage goes dark. The lights return on Eve and Oliver who unfreeze. Eve keeps munching on her apple, staring at Oliver and smiling to herself. Oliver feels very uncomfortable.

Eve: (Teasingly) Do I scare you, Ollie?

Oliver: No. And it's Oliver, I didn't say you could call me Ollie.

Oliver keeps fiddling with the couch.

Oliver: I wonder when Chloe will be back.

Eve: Oh, she'll be back soon. She's having her world turned upside down at this very moment.

Oliver: What? (Concerned) Eve…are you high? You're acting weird.

Eve laughs, puts the apple down on the table, claps her hands together, sits back in her chair and pouts at Oliver.

Eve: You're a good actor, Oliver Atreides. But not enough to fool me. I can see into your heart, and I see…terrible pain.

Oliver feels unnerved by her gaze but does his best to play it unbothered and laughs.

Oliver: I need whatever you're on. Xanny?

Eve: You thought you would feel better after you killed Adam. But it only made you feel worse. You tell yourself that you'll do anything to make Chloe happy, and you would, but at what price?

Chloe and Jason's part of the stage lights up and they unfreeze. Chloe stares at him in shock.

Chloe: You, you were there? You…you're part of the cult?

Jason: Not quite. I was told to take the photos by someone who is part of it. They thought your father had become too much of a liability and too greedy for power. I'm sorry Chloe, what they do is wrong, and I refuse to take part in that kind of thing, but going against them would not only kill my career but probably end up killing me too.

Chloe: So you're their fucking lapdog then? A good little boy who does what he's told and turns a blind eye, huh?

Jason: It's not so simple. Some of us have hard lives Chloe, some of us have a family relying on us that we have to look after, brothers and sisters to feed and hopefully send to college one day… don't be bitter, it worked out for both of us. With my help, you and your brother got away with murdering your dad… and we also had our fun, didn't we?

Chloe shakes her head in disbelief.

Chloe: Fuck you.

Jason smirks bitterly.

Jason: You're just upset I broke up with you before you could break up with me. It was never going to last. You'd have been on to the next guy now the case is over - someone richer, someone who fits better into your Upper East Side life.

Chloe: (Sadly and softly) I have no life, Jason.

Chloe folds her arms and hugs herself while she looks at her feet. When she looks back up at Jason, she has tears in her eyes. She stretches out a hand.

Chloe: Go on then, give me the list.

Oliver and Eve's part of the stage lights up. They unfreeze.

Eve: You see her face every time you close your eyes. The drugs help you sleep, but you can't sleep away your entire life. You get up in the morning for Chloe, for the soup kitchen you volunteer at, for the looks on stranger's faces when you give them random gifts of kindness and you think to yourself:

'Maybe God, just maybe, I can be a good person.'

And then you go back to your bed at night, eat as many sleeping pills as you can and imagine you're far away from your miserable life, that you're just a shepherd named Eric, who spends his days wandering the Swiss Mountains, eating swiss cheese, raising a family (three little girls) in a rustic pine-wood cottage near Lake Lucerne. You dream of it desperately but you're too embarrassed to admit it to any of your friends, you're too embarrassed to even admit it to Chloe, but deep down, once all this is over, once Chloe has settled into her role as CEO of Atreides and Co., like she wants, you dream of leaving your entire life behind you, starting a new life in Switzerland, being just a normal guy.

Oliver: (Freaking out) How the fuck could you know all of that? I've never told a soul.

Chloe and Jason's part of the stage lights up.

Jason hesitates as he is about to hand over the letter to Chloe.

Jason: Remember that I'm giving you this because you asked me, because I did enjoy my time with you, and because I do think that you deserve to know the truth. But if you tell anyone else Chloe, if you make it known that I gave you this list of names, I swear that I'll kill you myself, before they have a chance to hurt me and my family.

Chloe: Nice. That's really fucking nice of you, Jason. It's how every girl wants to get dumped – given a present and then a murder threat. Well done, really mature and friendly. Gold fucking star to you. (She makes a 'give it here' gesture) I'm waiting.

Jason: I warn you, you might not like what you see.

Jason hands Chloe the list and leaves. We see Chloe's eyes widen as she sees the names written there, she drops the paper in shock when she sees the final name on the list.

Chloe: (Shaking her head) No, no, no

She falls to the ground and checks the paper again. Her part of the stage goes dark. Oliver and Eve unfreeze.

Eve: (Continuing) You want to be a dad. You want to be the best dad to your daughters; you hope it will make up for what you've done, that Jenny's soul will forgive you.

Oliver: (With tears in his eyes) I don't understand.

Eve: You didn't believe in the supernatural until that night, until you saw me there.

Can you tell me why I was there, Oliver?

Oliver shakes his head, terrified.

Eve: You summoned me, baby…maybe this will jog your memory.

The lights become red and jarring. Creepy, cultish music plays out. Oliver holds his head in his hands as if he's in pain. Eve magically materialises a satanic mask and throws it at Oliver. He sees it, screams, accidentally knocks over the coffee table and backs away to the other side of the room.

Oliver: You are the Grand master?!

Eve: No, don't insult me. This is the garb of those who worship me, it is what you wore.

Oliver: Worship you? You can't be serious. I must be hallucinating. (He laughs hysterically and rubs his eyes). This is just a nightmare; I'll wake up at any moment now.

He closes his eyes and gently hits his face repeatedly while telling himself to wake up. Eve laughs.

Eve: You are very unlucky Oliver Atreides. Painfully so. But aren't you lucky to have met me face to face? (She winks at him.) Many people don't get the privilege, while they are in human form anyway.

Oliver holds himself and starts rocking backwards and forwards.

Oliver: Oh my God, I must be having a mental breakdown. We both must be.

Eve rolls her eyes.

Eve: Oh, I am perfectly sane, and I wouldn't bother trying to invoke the other one (She points up to the sky) Adam, Bill, Sandra, they all belong to me. I have fulfilled my obligation; it is only a matter of time before I take your soul, and your sister's.

Oliver: I don't believe you. You're not…

Eve: Say it. Say my name, sweetie. Well, one of my real names.

Oliver: But …you're, you're a woman! And you called yourself Eve! Why would you do that?

Eve: Because it's funny. "Adam and Eve". (She chuckles to herself.) It made fucking your dad quite the ironic experience. He never realised who I was, of course, my disguise was perfect.

She turns a hard eye on Oliver and gets serious.

It worked perfectly on all of you... never doubt the arrogance of mankind, there's nothing more deliciously stupid than a human who thinks he can manipulate the primordial forces of this world. A world that was born of me. A world that shall die with me.

She smiles.

Time to go. I shall see you again child, I am sure. The sins of the fathers shall be visited upon the sons and the sins of the sons upon their fathers. From Greece to America thousands of years later and you still haven't changed. How many lifetimes will it take for you Atreides to escape your cyclic violence? It tires me. Now that's saying something.

The lights become red and frantic once again, representing Eve's magic and Oliver's deteriorating state of mind. During this, Oliver curls into a ball on the floor in shock, while Eve disappears. The lights return to normal as Chloe appears in the doorway, in tears, holding the list that Jason gave her.

Chloe: Oliver.

Oliver breaks out of his reverie and looks up at Chloe as the lights fade away.

End of scene.

Scene 2: Oliver's Lament

Chloe sits prim and proper on the sofa. She remains silent for the whole scene. Oliver stands in front of her.

N.B.: When Oliver 'talks to the audience' during this scene, he's really staring into space, talking to Chloe, himself and God. He doesn't interact with the audience like Eve does when she talks to them.

Oliver: It was Monday the 15th of September 2008. I was woken up by a phone call from my friend Zac, he told me that the Lehman Brothers had just declared bankruptcy. We went down Wall Street to see the exodus from their headquarters. Hundreds of people walking out with all their stuff in boxes.

An investment bank, like ours. It was a terrible vision of what was going to happen to us.

I tried calling dad all day, but he didn't pick up and he wasn't at the office either. Two days later, I got a call from Bill; he told me to drive down immediately to this fancy mansion upstate, and that he and dad would speak to me when they arrived there that night. I thought it was some country retreat, and that it was odd that dad wanted to go there when we needed to be in New York to deal with the crisis, (bitterly) but I always did what dad told me too, and so I went. I nearly got lost on the way there, the house was surrounded by miles and miles of private woods. When I arrived at the front gate and told the receptionist my name, ten minutes later a butler came out to meet me. He said that I had to leave my car and be blindfolded if I wanted to enter. I thought that dad must have sent me to... an orgy or something...(sheepishly) so I agreed to the blindfold.

(He laughs shortly, embarrassed at himself, and rubs his neck)

I knew it wasn't the time to be doing that. But... I was a jackass back then, and we'd had a rough couple months at the office, I hardly remembered the last time I had a break. I went in and we walked for what must have been twenty minutes till we reached the house, then I got taken up to a bedroom and my blindfold was taken off. There was no orgy, just a normal room. The butler apologised for the secrecy and said that it was the tradition of the host. He asked me to ring the bell if I needed anything and that my dad would be there soon. I thought it was all very fucking weird and wondered if I'd been kidnapped but tried to stay calm. I called Bill and he explained that it was his friend's house and that I had to be blindfolded because I wasn't one of 'the club' yet, he said that he would explain everything with dad when they arrived... When they did arrive a couple hours later, they looked horrible, it was the first time in my life I saw dad crying...

(Flashback)

Adam: It's a fucking disaster. There's nothing else to say. We are going to be the next Lehman brothers. I'll have to declare bankruptcy by the end of the week unless a miracle comes to save us.

Bill: Millions and millions of Americans' life savings are going to be lost, no one wants to buy us out, and the government has refused to do anything to help.

Adam: Son, we're about to lose everything…and I can't even repay all the debt I owe, I may as well shoot myself.

Oliver: Don't say that. Is there absolutely nothing we can do?

Adam and Bill share a look.

Bill: There is one thing. Your father and I have discussed it, but we won't do it unless you agree.

Freeze.

Oliver: (to the audience) He went on to tell me about occult activity, I thought he was insane.

Unfreeze.

Oliver: (to Bill) You're seriously trying to tell me that magic is real?

Adam: Don't be so ignorant. Do you really think that in thousands of years of human history, every time people practised black magic, they were just idiots making it up? No, black magic was more accepted in the past, and people knew better how to use it; it was part of daily life.

Bill: But now, this knowledge only belongs to a select few and those who wish to seek it out…Oliver, if you absolutely had to pick between the left button which drops a ginormous wrecking ball on one man and the right button which drops the same wrecking ball but on five men, which button would you choose?

Oliver: (Hesitantly) I guess…I'd have to choose the left.

Adam: Exactly. Sometimes we are forced to pick the lesser of two evils. Sometimes we have to do one bad thing, so that a lot of good can follow.

Oliver: What are you suggesting?

Adam looks down at his hands.

Bill: One life. Sacrificing one life, in order to save many from being ruined.

Oliver stares at them in shock.

Oliver: (Horrified) Human sacrifice?

Oliver protests and tries to leave the room, Adam and Bill hold him back and stop him from leaving.

Bill: Listen, it's how these things work. It's about energies. Exchanging one thing for another. We're asking the spirits to save us from utter financial ruin and poverty, maybe even your dad's suicide, all of that is a lot to ask for, and requires a lot in return... a life.

Oliver starts protesting but is interrupted by Adam.

Adam: We aren't murderers, Oliver. We're people with good intentions in tough times. Our bank is something greater than any of us. It's... the mothership, and if we let her sink, think of all those passengers that are going to drown along with us. It's the normal people of the US who are going to feel the effects of the financial crisis the worst. Millions of life savings, pensions and jobs are going to be lost, including all the charities and institutions that get the majority of their funding from us. If you had the opportunity to save all those lives, how could you not take it?

Oliver: Simple. I don't want to murder anyone, dad.

Bill: In life things don't happen the way you want them to. You can't have everything, Oliver, something has to be sacrificed. The life that we propose taking in the ritual, has been very carefully selected: she's a prostitute, a heroin addict with no family, no friends, and she's got HIV. No one will miss her, and she'll probably be dead in five years' time anyway.

Oliver stares at him, disgusted.

Adam: (Calmly) Oliver, look at me.

Oliver obeys.

Do you have any idea, what it's like to be poor?

Oliver shakes his head.

(Calmly) No, you fucking don't.

We have so much debt attached to our name that it will become a stain on Wall Street. No one else is going to employ you. You'll end up having to work at McDonalds, I'm being serious. Tax? That's something you'll actually have to pay. Do you really think you'll be able to survive in the real world? You've never even seen a washing machine with your own eyes, let alone used one! You grew up so blessed and so fortunate that you, and especially your sisters, won't be able to survive having that all taken away. Do you think that Chloe will be able to cope in the real world? (Adam laughs) Give me a break.

Oliver: Chloe has Randy. He supports her financially.

Bill shakes his head.

Bill: Randy McDowell is tied up with our finances.

Oliver: (to Adam) Then why the hell did you make Chloe marry him? I thought, I thought the whole point of the marriage was to financially secure us, worst comes to worst! You even threatened Chloe that you'd take Jenny out of school if she didn't agree!

Adam: Their marriage was more for.... political reasons. Randy wanted her, and I owed Randy.

Oliver looks at him, disgusted.

Adam: I know, Oliver. You can blame me for it later, but right now we don't have the time (pause)...one life, for millions and millions of people's lives, for their futures. Their children's futures. Your sisters' futures. You decide.

(End of flashback.)

Oliver: (to the audience) I was an idiot. I really believed that I was doing the best thing out of a terrible situation. One life versus millions. But it's never that simple.... I should've known better than to think I could judge the worth of one life over another.

Beat.

And Karma came back to bite me for it.

He cries.

(Said through his tears) I hardly remember what happened that night. I got given these drugs that made me...I thought there was a white deer running around, and I was hunting it. There were all these faces in masks that were hunting it with me.

Chloe puts her head in her hands.

There was a pentagram made of fire, on the ground, that seared the whites of my eyes, and the rain…it was thick and red, it felt like blood…that's all I remember. It never leaves me, though I've tried so hard to forget.

When I woke up the next morning, in the woods, I was covered in blood. I was the only one there. There was nothing and no one else around me, I felt terrified, I didn't stay to look around. I ran back to the house and rang the doorbell, the same butler met me, he didn't look surprised. He got me cleaned up, I saw no one else in the house. He gave me my phone and there was a text from Bill. Just two words. 'It worked.'

Around a week later, on September 29th, the stock market crashed…but our bank remained safe. Our stocks even started rising, I tried to forget what I'd been part of.

He sobs and shakes his head.

But then three days later you texted me, Chloe, saying that (he trembles) Jenny's boarding school reported her missing. I called dad, I texted him, but there was nothing. Same with Bill. I drove round to dad's house to confront him about it but was told he was too busy to talk to me. He wasn't at the office either. I started to get this sinking, horrible feeling inside, that something was very, very wrong…a week later her body was found all the way in Virginia, three miles from her school.

Call it a brother's intuition, but I just knew it had to be related to what happened. But I still didn't want to believe it. Dad had told me a hooker would be the ritual victim not…he couldn't have done, I thought, he wouldn't have done. The same day you and I went to identify her body at the police station, I dropped you off home, then I finally got to speak to dad and Bill, which I hadn't done since that night…dad couldn't look me in the eye.

(Flashback):

Oliver storms into the room where Adam and Bill are sitting.

Oliver: (To Adam) Why haven't you been picking up my calls?

Silence.

Why weren't you at the police station today?

Silence.

I had to see my sister's body. Ripped apart.

Why weren't you there?

(Screaming) Why weren't you there?

Adam puts his head in his hands. Bill tries to calm Oliver down while Oliver starts speaking the next few lines.

Oliver: (Hysterical) Something doesn't feel right. Why is she dead after...don't tell me, don't tell me...you gave me all those drugs, I, I remember hunting a deer, but, but it was actually the ritual victim, that poor, poor girl, the hooker, right? It was the hooker, right?

Bill shakes his head, with tears in his eyes.

Bill: We're sorry we had to lie, Oliver.

Oliver shakes his head, in denial.

Oliver: No, no…no! Dad. (Screaming) Look at me!

Adam doesn't. Oliver rushes forward and tries to beat him up. Bill pins his arms behind him. Oliver screams and cries. Bill holds him and cries with him. Adam winces at the sound of his son screaming in agony and fails to hold back his tears.

Adam: This ritual required the biggest sacrifice in order to work. I loved her more than all of you combined. You don't know how much it hurt me to do what I did.

Oliver: (Sobbing hysterically) You made me kill Jenny?!!

He screams in pain.

Adam: It was my duty, for the family, for my blood, the Atriedes. I will never, ever, let her sacrifice go to waste.

Adam leaves the room in tears, while Bill holds Oliver back.

(End of flashback.)

Oliver: Dad immediately had me flown over to a mental health institution in Europe so that I wouldn't try to kill him. That's why I was really there for six months, it wasn't just to help me out of my depression. I thought about many things while I was there… suicide mainly. But every time I came close, my therapist would remind me that I still had a sister alive, also grieving, who needed me, and how would she feel if she had to lose both her siblings in one year…When I was stable enough, I came back to New York. And your face was the first face I saw when I came out of airport security. (He smiles) You looked so happy to see me, Chloe. (He smiles again through his tears) I'll never forget how you looked at me. It was like God giving me a hug for the first time in ages.

His smile drops. He goes sit by Chloe's feet.

You don't know how much I regret it… I can never, ever forgive myself. I ruined my life. (Looks at Chloe) I ruined my life forever. I never should have agreed to joining that ritual. I killed her and I also killed myself…I'm sorry Chloe, I'm sorry that I couldn't bring myself to tell you.

I don't expect you to forgive me. You can send that list of all the cult members who participated in Jenny's murder to the press. Including my name. We should all be in jail; I'll go willingly. But please, just tell me, tell me that there's something I could do, something I could do that was good. That was truly good. That I could work towards earning your forgiveness… and God's. I'll do anything, anything… I made

a mistake…that will haunt me and torture me forever…but…
I still want to be a good person. I want to be a good person,
Chloe.

He puts his hands on her knees and cries into them.

Pause.

Chloe softly, but firmly, removes her brother's hands, folds
them together, then gets up and leaves the room coldly and
silently. Oliver is absolutely heartbroken.

End of scene.

Scene 3: Judgement Day

The stage is cleared from the previous scene. We are back in the Atreides family graveyard. When the lights come up, there are now two gravestones placed next to each other – Jenny and Oliver. Eve walks to centre stage with two red roses.

Eve: (to the audience) What did you think of that? Would you have forgiven Oliver? Or left him in the cold dust like his beloved sister did?

She looks at Oliver's grave.

He was found three days later, holding Jenny's gravestone. He'd had an overdose…. That made it 4 out of 5 for me. Although… something tells me that Eric will see those Swiss slopes much sooner than he anticipated.

(She smirks) I would be lying if I said that I'm sorry for not being honest with you about who I am. It's hard to keep yourself entertained for millennia and millennia. People never change, so it's just the same job over and over and over again. I have to find little ways to amuse myself otherwise it gets tedious.

Chloe walks up to the gravestones with two bouquets of white roses.

Here's little Miss Perfect. You know, part of me wishes she'd surprise me. It's exceedingly rare when I lose and winning used to fill me with insatiable pleasure. But as my darling Oscar Wilde used to say, pleasure is very different from happiness. (She shrugs) What can you do, then, but laugh at it all?

Eve composes herself into her Eve persona and then walks up to Chloe with a forlorn look.

Eve: I am so, so sorry.

Chloe turns around and smiles sadly.

Chloe: Thank you, Eve.

Eve places a rose on each grave and then stands in line with Chloe. They both stare at the gravestones.

Eve: At least now they can be together, forever.

Chloe wipes away a tear. Eve gives her a side hug and Chloe rests her head on Eve's shoulder. They stand there for a moment before Eve breaks the silence.

Eve: But I also must congratulate you, both on your oncoming divorce and your appointment as the new CEO of Atreides and Co.

Chloe smiles, lifts her head talks to Eve face to face.

Chloe: Thank you so much. It has not been easy, but I think there is a vague light at the end of the tunnel. Jenny would want me to keep going.

Eve: And Oliver. He loved you dearly.

Chloe wears an unreadable expression. She doesn't say anything, only nods politely. There's a short pause.

Chloe: (Wistfully but very sadly) You know… in Ancient Greece they used to publicly mourn aloud, wail for days, and it was normal… I wish we could do that; it would help release the pain. People expect you to be over your grief in about six months…then you're supposed to go back to normal. But you never do, you just grieve inside, for the rest of your life.

Eve nods in understanding with a thoughtful expression (no sarcasm yet).

Eve: You grieve for Oliver now too.

Chloe looks sadly at his grave.

Chloe: My brother was a very, very complicated person. He had sides to him even I was unaware of, and in the end, (bitterly) he turned out to be just like Adam.

Eve: No.

Chloe looks at her.

No, I don't think he was the one like Adam.

Chloe laughs bitterly, pretending not to understand Eve's meaning.

Chloe: Well, who else?

She clears her throat and tries to change the subject.

Chloe: You know, I haven't seen you at Church in a while, didn't you say that you used to go?

Eve: When I see people as devoted as you there, I just feel too inadequate to come in.

Chloe: God is a fair judge to all of us, he welcomes us all with an open heart.

Eve: You are obviously an expert on the word of God. I've known a lot of righteous people just like you.

Chloe: You are too kind.

Eve smiles and tries not to laugh. Chloe doesn't notice. Eve then looks around the graveyard.

Eve: Did you bury Adam and Sandra here?

Chloe: My father is buried at the back of the garden, near where we keep the trash. I would have given him an unmarked grave if I could, but that would've looked suspicious. Sandra, the scheming bitch, actually made a will, despite being so young, and asked to be buried with Adam. I didn't allow that of course. I sent her away to one of her sister's.

Eve nods.

Eve: 'Forgive, as the lord forgave you.' Colossians 3:13. But not for everyone right? Though I wonder if God would forgive you for poisoning Sandra and the baby.

Chloe stares at her, alarmed.

Chloe: Eve, Sandra died of a sudden heart attack. It was shock.

Eve: You don't need be defensive with me, my love, I'm your friend. You used the poison I offered you to use on Adam. (She smiles conspiratorially and leans in) Don't worry, I won't tell a soul, cross my heart, hope to die.

Chloe gets lost in Eve's eyes momentarily but then gathers herself together, Eve smirks at her reaction and holds her hand.

Eve: I have a soft spot for you, Chloe. You have such an unwavering sense of self-belief. It reminds me of myself. (She smiles warmly) I'm sure that now you are CEO, you'll use your newfound power to do the right thing and stop your bank from continuing to be involved with all those sweatshops, prostitution, trafficking, and drug rings, under the humble cloak of its charity work, of course.

Chloe removes her hand from Eve's, shocked at her frankness. She quickly glances around and smiles politely.

Chloe: Being CEO, you're under the weight of millions depending on you. My team is investigating it, but don't worry Eve, my bank will not engage nor support any practices which harm the vulnerable and less fortunate. 'Blessed are the meek, for they shall inherit the earth.'

Eve: (enthusiastically) Yes, quite right!! Especially blessed when something like Adam and Bill's satanic cult no longer exists. When are we going to leak the pictures to the press? And the list of names?

Pause.

Chloe: Eve, I'm sorry. But I don't think that's a good idea.

Eve pretends to be surprised/ Eve secretly smiles.

Eve: You decided to turn a blind eye?

Chloe: (defensively) No, not a blind eye, but it would put both of our lives in danger, and what use would that be to the world? There's no point dying a martyr, not when I have plenty of work to do - most importantly lots of charities to support, including ones that support other young women and children.

Chloe touches Eve's arm sadly.

It is a tragedy, an absolute tragedy, and believe me when I say how painful it is to make this decision, but I just cannot help those poor victims of the cult. (She shrugs helplessly) At least they're usually prostitutes, maybe if they went to Church instead of selling their bodies, they wouldn't find themselves caught up with all of that.

She touches her cross.

I will pray for them.

Eve starts laughing, it grows louder and louder. Chloe stares, surprised, finding her behaviour odd and rude.

Chloe: (curtly) What's the matter?

Eve, still laughing, manages to compose herself.

Eve: Nothing, I just have one question…

She takes out a red apple and gently tosses it once up and down in her hand, then she holds it out to Chloe.

Eve: Do you believe in Judgement Day?

Eve smiles.

The lights fade away to black.

THE END.

Printed in Great Britain
by Amazon

ca88b2ba-e1e7-43df-814b-a56c9404e87bR02